Our Big Island

Frané Lessac and Mark Greenwood

Artbeat
Publishers

An ocean adventure began
on this day,
sailing from Sydney past
Botany Bay.
Uncle Max stood on deck in
Captain's regalia
with nautical charts and
a map of Australia.

The Captain and his crew of four
set sail around the island's shore,
Cody, Napuru, Nangala and Sheila,
his brave shipmates and a little blue heeler.

In Bass Strait they hit mountainous seas,
storm sails billowed in the blustery breeze.
The wooden boat pitched and rolled with the motion
of whitecaps, breakers and the furious ocean.

Penguins paraded in battered bays,
old hideouts of smugglers and castaways.
The Twelve Apostles stood tall in the night.
Ahead was the Great Australian Bight.

Constellations clustered in the velvet sky.

Napuru held a sextant up to one eye.

They navigated by compass, the Moon and Mars,

the Milky Way and heavenly stars.

From bunks below deck
the shipmates rose,
as Uncle Max called out,
"Thar she blows !"
Shadows surfaced with
misty spouts
exposing huge white
calloused snouts.
They breached and sounded,
splashing their tails.
A majestic sight were the
southern right whales .

At the Batavia Coast they dived to explore
sunken ships on the dark ocean floor.
Broken by storms and tumbling waves,
old wrecks lay silent in watery graves.

Carried by the current they drifted to pass
dugongs grazing on undersea grass.
In crystal waters they anchored to admire
the bottlenose dolphins at Monkey Mia.

The Indian ocean was
turquoise blue
at the coral reef called Ningaloo.
Captain and crew snorkelled
and swam
over brain coral, starfish
and giant clam.
They came upon a great
whale shark
as it glided through the
wild marine park.

Near Broome with the rising and falling tides
they saw dinosaur tracks the sea often hides.
Old luggers cruised by the rugged red shore,
on a search for pearls from the ocean floor.

They sailed to the Gulf through the Arafura sea.
A maze of mangroves stretched endlessly.
Through an old spyglass they watched in awe
as crocodiles lurked on the muddy shore.

Around Thursday Island
they steered the ship
and on Friday sighted
Cape York's tip.
They watched turtles on
a seasonal quest
struggle up the beach to
burrow a nest.

Tropical waters at the Great Barrier Reef
were a divers' dream world beyond belief.
They explored coves and coral cays,
island havens and secluded bays.

Along the Sunshine Coast the high seas rolled
under a twilight sky of crimson and gold.
The crew set sail in the spray and foam,
"All hands on deck for the voyage home!"

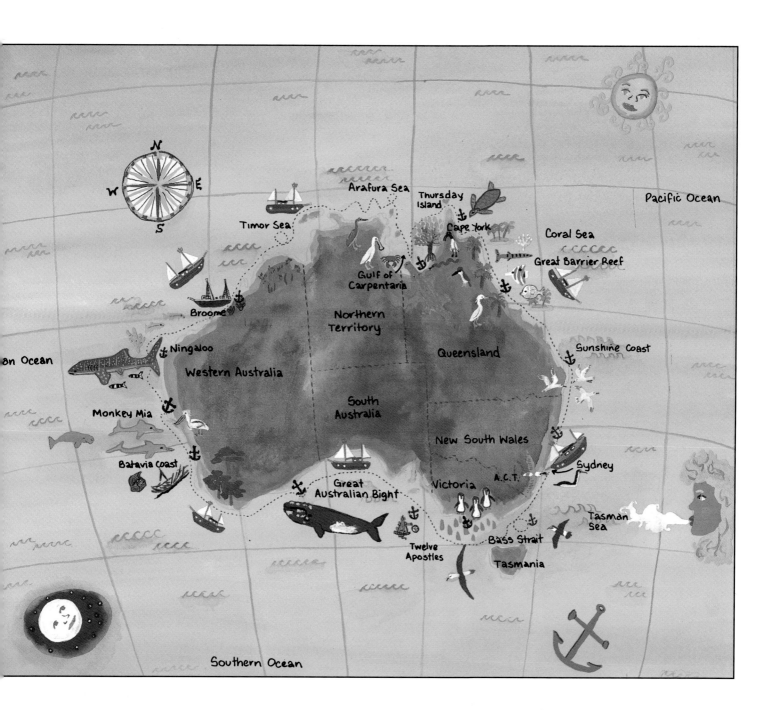

First published 1995
Reprinted 2002 by ARTBEAT PUBLISHERS
PO Box 1110 Fremantle, Western Australia 6160
Telephone +61 (08)9430 5479 Facsimile +61 (08) 9431 7754
Email: artbeat@ozemail.com.au   www.artbeatpublishers.com

ISBN 0-9579551-0-3 (paperback)

Other titles from Artbeat Publishers:
Magic Boomerang
Outback Adventure